"Once A Lover Always A Fool"

Philani Amadéus Nyoni

All rights reserved. No part of this publication shall be reproduced in any form you can imagine without my explicit permission. Things might get ugly...seriously.

©Philani Amadéus Nyoni 2012

The Light Pages

When We Meet Again...

Things we regret most are the chances we never took,
Those we love most are those that we forsook.
I don't believe in living in regret,
So since I am not dead yet
When we meet again
There will be rain…

I will gaze deep into your bewildering eyes;
Then to relinquish my heart's silent cries
I will tell you how I truly feel.
As an oath that the words are real
I will kiss your soft sweet lips
Where sacred water slips...

Her Sweetness

I know a sweet miss so divine
She told me 'Sir, my heart is thine.'
I smiled and told her that is fine
For she in turn holds mine.

At once the world was lost, remote
Her lips to me became a note,
The fairest poem ever written
Which had me quickly smitten.

I laid my hands upon her hips,
I shut my eyes and turned to kiss
Those sweet, rosy, petalled lips
From which sweet nectar drips.

O my sweet miss did not protest,
She urged me forward in my quest
With the softness of her breast
Pressing up against my chest!

For her I cast all fears aside,
Forever let this love abide;
If this be a form of suicide
Then in my tomb you will discover
A dead man smiling at his lover!

Princess S.

That first glance,
Face's radiance, mace in my eyes,
Now behold a glimpse
Of eternal existence,
Immortal dance,
Evermore never the less
This day hence I owe my years
To you, bonny lass.
Trance, hold me, lasso,
Lace my solace lanced heart,
Bless yesterday's curse,
Let's trace my countenance
In the depths of your skirts.
Countess, virtues countless,
Essence priceless, Ageless' excess.

Eye of Heaven

By the eye of heaven I swear,
Before you all my soul lies bare.
Of the thousand rhymes my pen once wrote
None was truer than this note.
Now I strip my Vulcan armour,
For you alone just you, none other.
Here I lay my heart at your feet,
Only a prayer stops you trampling it.
This verse is my dirge, in your eyes
My form is sealed, lips too tell no lies
Like promises to others of my love,
Bear witness moon and sun above!
Captor of my heart from the first moment,
Receive my heart with this false sonnet.

Teach Me

My soul leaps to the tune of your lips,
In your whisper I sway like the lily by the brook;
Enchanted by the snaking rhythm of your steps
I follow religiously. Many deities, See how I forsook
Them to be baptised in your kiss? Now teach this pen
To mirror your excellence, not for my honour among men
But only to content this throbbing in my vein;
How can I love you with all I am if I cannot
Transcribe the immortal truth that lies in your eye?
Teach me the tongues that the fallen forgot,
Tame my hand and never again shall I lie
Through similes and metaphors of angels and roses;
Then when that force beneath your breast
Mutinies I will give breath back to you from the voices
That sleep in my pages in momentary rest.

Pledge of My Heart...

Now listen to my pledge:
This night forth 'til a dirge
Is sung over Your sleeping corpse
I shall be the matter of Your hopes,
Dreams, visions and fantasies.
Yours from me are oceans and seas
In the land where water is love.
Listen intently to the cooing dove,
He sings the song retrieved
From the depth of my heart deprived
Of a voice. Unintelligible as it may sound,
It is inspired by emotion found
Deep within me. Words are an attempt
And a failure. They cannot content
Me when employed to tell of my fire
That bears livid flames of desire
Enthralled. My wants are tamed by inability;
I want things that are far from possibility,
Like to climb to heaven and bring You the moon
As a pledge of my love; but in no time soon
Or ever shall I fulfil this. I'll only say
That on each and every passing day
Phoebus rides across the sky
I will be there for each tear You cry,
I will be there to kiss them away, trade them for the night
Throughout which I will whisper into Your ear
The Pledge of My Heart.

A Midnight Dance

She sweeps her skirts my gaze to win
The stars have crowned her queen;
She flirts with earth, the wind, my gaze-
The gazelle exudes less grace.

Clothed in night and rising dust
Too thin to shelter lust,
The roaring drum ignites a trance
She bleeds her sweat in dance.

She beams beneath the thick moonlight
While lusty eyes delight,
Worshipping her every part
In the unforbidding night.

I lay my claim with an eye's invite
Then melt into the dark,
She follows me beyond the lake
And lays her flesh at stake.

I cup her pointy cones now bare
Retreat I do not dare,
Then take her on the riverbed
Like Adam newly wed!

Tonight we burn the coal of night
And roast in sweet moonlight,
'til amber breaks the morning sky
In unison we lie.

The Battle of Eden

Gentle with your weight on me my Love;
Do not crush me with Your love.
Gentle rain soothes the torso…
Let it rain, let there be rain.
To beasts we evolve; Your pouncing form
I am the prey. Consume me in the rain…
We grunt like them too, beasts at war:
On this immortal night shall the flesh of the
Predator feed the prey, nature is defied.
Rain stops…but the beasts still wrestle,
Canine fury, desire fuelling, the fiery hearse
Of Elijah burnt much less, canines…canines…
The forest trembles…entangled with each other,
The beasts tumble…forest tremble beasts tumble…
This is not a war with daughters of Satan though
Many of them I have battled; I bear the marks
Of their talons still, their fangs and poison
In their saliva. This is the Battle of Truth, no
Secrets between, naked truths with common
Barricade being the sheet of sky.
It is the battle of Eden, warrior HE
And Amazon SHE evolved to beasts.
Forest stop trembling, beasts stop tumbling,
Eyes of passion are locked in stillness,
Bound in each other's awe they do not move,
They lose sense of the moment, lose the
Urgency of battle: that flesh must be penetrated
Where hunger has laid the stakes.

The tumble ceases, his claws are drawn to pounce,
She snarls. The Panther opens his mouth to consume her…
More rain…rain…rain…

The Battle of Eden II

This battle has lasted long now,
From beneath the fur the sweat permeates.
They might as well have become snakes, Recall;
This is the battle of Eden.
Snakes! Serpents I say! Slithering, sliding
In the martial embrace men adapted and called judo.
Lockdown, nature's chains, the fiends of Eden
Upon each other unleashed, such fury, such passion…
Is there a greater taboo?!
They slither and slide consumed by the mutual thought:
Consume the other…consume the other…consume…

The female is wounded…her breathing heightens,
She is battling for air, turns her head to the side,
Her fiery eyes dim and roll back,
She arches her back involuntarily…twitching…
She no longer breathes but ejects staccato pieces of her soul…
The life of a deity, a goddess is slain!
But the killer too is on the bank of Styx.
Exhaustion of the passion has drained him almost dry,
The last shots on their way home…He never knew a greater
foe,
One whose death cost him his life as well…
Collapse…nothing moves, the death of two immortals freezes
time…
The heaving beasts have honoured the fire in their hearts,
Fed it with sinew, flesh and self, it has consumed them.
Feel the ejection of their souls in unison to mingle in the air
And henceforth be known as Wind. Love; we made it my love.

Flower, The Rising Sun

Sweat of the night drenches the morning earth
While the Sun quietly blooms from my bed.
God sent Her kiss to revive my breath,
Gone are the nights I wished I was dead!
I smell the Flower while Her rays penetrate
My gloom. My heart has found few joys in this life,
But the nectar in Her kiss has changed my state.
Scent of morning in my nostrils bridging the gulf
Between joy and life, won't you show me eternity
That we may live it through, or teach me to host
Your glowing heart until all my reality
Dims when my last die is finally cast?
In your golden light I am Pharaoh never to rust.

Cradle From The Grave

Caress me lover in your fold
And shield me from the cold,
Hold me in your arms today
And make me swear to stay.

Hold me close all through the winter,
O make the sour sweeter,
So that when that summer comes
I will recall your charms.

I will recall your charms my miss
I will remember this,
Remember that when I was cold
Your heart was flaming gold,

Remember that the death of Sun
Could hardly spell me done,
You for me were always there
When no one seemed to care.

Remember that you loved me when
I was not half the man
That destiny sought me to be
But yet you stayed with me.

Red Phoenix

Hot-headed-red-haired fiend burnt my flesh and scorched my
heart.
Red was the colour of her love, red I saw on my part.
She was an enchanting little devil
Who erected statues in the loins of angels,
Had eyes like the sun that rose behind painted clouds.
Her ass was on fire like a phoenix burning to the ground;
Flaming meteorite, she fell from the sky, I am most certain
The planet she hailed from is Saturn,
Lord of the Rings. I wanted to marry her among other things,
But she felled my poetry, now count the rings…
From a simple compliment, 'You as hot as hell'
She left me with one hell of a story to tell.
We made love every night, consumed mutual lust
That burnt pillows and sheets, melted iron and rust.
The passion she would ignite with her fiery tongue
Burnt nightlong to the last bit of oxygen in my lung,
Caged in the volcanic crevices of her bosom I was her lover
Until she spat me onto the pavement like a globe of saliva.
Long story short, like hell I was burnt,
And missing her like hell my days were spent.
She turned my heart to stone and paved the way for You
Because Your first kiss was a drink of morning dew.
I guess what I am trying to say
Is that I went through hell to get to heaven.

Bear With Me…

Bear with me, this fragile heart
Was reclaimed from Your ancestors,
Barbarians in skirts by whose blade I bled half past dead.
I have forgotten how to love so bear with me, this lonely shell
Was hardened by war that their arms may harm me no more,
Their kisses their lies and the likes, their boomerang smiles
Sent to retrieve my heart went back empty,
Bear with me I forgot how to love.
But the east is where the sun rises, even in Japan,
Thus love is where love is found:
Here, where dead hearts found life.
Love is where daggers fly when strangers lie:
But let not my hand nor yours deal in blades,
Mortality's loan is too short to spend on wrath
And blood. May we defile the tombs of Juliet and her beau;
Defecate upon their legacy to write Lovers' Book anew,
Thorough the iron gates of time to upset Marvell,
Turn his decayed mistress green 'til she is coy no more!
Spit fire upon the sun that his days may be long,
Our years longer and our joys the longest,
Then clocks be broken and time stopped…
Your lips to mine engaged, may we know the pleasures
That Adam and Eve refused, passion upon this bed nightly
made
Ignites the perverts of the sky to peep through the black glass
above, I see them, the moon too wide eyed!
Upon this bed I lay my love,
By the mingling of your breath with mine
New life is begotten of us both.
May he not inherit his father's deceitful ways which he forgot
When you taught him how to love again.

Mother And Child

Upon this breast where I lie the rest of night
May life be given to the one not yet born.
Within those hands my great delights,
Quiet my little one when he moans.
Within these hands the envy of scribes
Let blisters run deep to feed mother and child
With more than meagre morsels and bribes
To see another day. Let survival escape the mind,
As my Father giveth unto me, freely I offer to my own:
Abundance. Upon your brow I command sweat,
Strain upon your back and a groan-
Only in pleasure, moan only for the sweet!
Then nothing more shall I require of you,
My quest for perfection is surely through.

The

dark

page

This Tinker Thought

Foreign frontiers, Fanakalo flirt,
Artillery aimed, Amadéus angles another apparent angel,
Partake piss, poisonous poetry permeates,
Rip rind, ravish richly, religion raped.

Counting comets climbing cloudless climes,
Distant dots denote dusk defeated day,
Heaving heart has held heaven,
Now nostalgic nightmares nest.

Long live livid love!
Sacrilegious sarcasm seeks scapegoat,
Battered bruised, bashed by bedevilling broods,
Wondering why we wander with witches.

Dear Memory

And what could I give for another night,
Waxed in moonlight the two of us,
Burning the coal of dark with livid passion?
From me through your lips it leapt; a spark,
While synchronised nakedness concluded Friction
And punctured the stillness with acute heaving.
I was yours and you were mine, measuring time
By the beads of sweat stringing into rivulets.
Trickling, they flowed into rivers drifting
Into a chasm where speech was poetry
And the drumming rhythm beneath your breast was pace.
That was then; who could have known it was the autumn of
our youth?
Suddenly the water is gone and
Time's coarse sands remain with the salt
On the banks where only memory could be saved when
reality prevailed.
In time it all turns to dust,
To dust like the widowed emotions within me!
Was it too much to ask; you mine without season,
Wedded unto Time until the very end?
It was the twilight of our youth and reality prevailed:

Your pen cannot write cheques!
'At least not yet!' I corrected.

While I'm heading there remind me not to wave at you, say hi,
Or stop for a little chit-chat and reminiscence-pie.
Remind me to forget you when I see you on the street,
And my whole being not to ache for your touch,
Your scent and a little feel of your exposed skin.
Remind me not to speak to you,
Lest I bleed my wallet for a taste of yesterday.
Remind me that what you are, killed what you were

To create what you will be
Since what you are doing 'is for a shot at college'.
Remind me that the red lights scorched the lover in you.
And I hope the sacrifice is worth it,
The path to heaven may cut through hell,
But those who left Egypt for Canaan never made it...

Adieu my love.

After Youth

And what shall become of you
When Time's hands have done their art?
Crayons of hue re-coloured you in shades of dusk,
Graffiti etched upon your brow,
Flawless grace reduced to caricature,
Once impeccable beauty redrawn abstract
And the stains of his oils mock your portraits?
His fingerprints plastered across the wall of your soul:
Your essence withered to the stench of pending death
And your confidence shaken to infirmity,
Shall these suitors, princes in Chevrolets -if not to dust
returned-
Still whistle their impotence through toothless smiles?
Bite deep into the flesh of youth but be wary of the stone,
Cast by those who perceive themselves sinless
Should three words thin to three letters.
I do not wish disease, pestilence or plague upon you,
Only true fruits of old age, regrets grown
To appreciation of possibilities
Chastised by the rod of Time for the road not taken,
Insolence blossomed to wisdom;
Blind valour to meditation.
Subtle pencil strokes to Time's masterpiece evolved,
While I on his easel remain a fool,
Loving you in more earnest than when I was a boy.

A Love With Seasons

Thunder quakes and lightning strikes
The Sky just one voice,
He calls beneath the grey blanket
She follows husband's noise.

Undress my love! His deep command;
The wind sweeps leaves away,
Mountains' rise oh Nature's thighs
The wind has left them bare!

Wind the finger of the Sky
Is weaving through her hair,
Their passion will leave Ivy green,
If only he would stay.

Darts of heaven, sperm of life
Nature's thighs receive,
Shoots are sprouting, flowers bloom
Time for him to leave…

Jungle music

Alone in the jungle,
Concrete.
Screaming within I yearn for her,
Come soon
I need you so.
I wait.
Time talks as it ticks.
I give up
And press on without you
While the ticks of time suck me dry.
An alleluia won't help right now,
My confession is due:
Here and now I renounce my shadow.
Martyr hanged with his rosary,
On love's stake I burned;
Inferno licks my skin
Bled my life through in vain,
So here I sit, concrete licking my cheeks,
Love's monkey tricks have me yearning
To be swallowed alive,
Send the church choir to rehearsal…

Written with Boitumelo Richard Nyoni

For A Blemished Rose

Tiny light seeping in let it not
Go to waste but be given to thought.
Scribbling beneath my shadow,
Racing the day chasing tomorrow,
Distant thoughts beg my pen's task
Ere the onset of tarnishing dusk.

What blooms too must wilt,
In mortality it's for death we were built.
I drank your dew in the morn,
Basked in your shade at noon,
My tears upon your petals beneath the moon.
Goodbye dear Flawa, between truth
And illusion You stood in my authored myth,
Here and now again my blemished
Rose I profess the divinity I cherished.
Your scar is deeper than my feeling,
Drown in yours I in mine, I am weary of reeling
For Your heavy heart.

Heaven's candle has burnt out…

The Solitude Of Poetry

A lover's breast I crave tonight,
A lover's song I yearn for now.
Journey wide, journey far, a lonely traveller I am,
A lonesome drifter, a tasteless spice in the seasons of time,
Yet mighty sinew in the bosom of rhyme.
Here we are, PAN and I, as it was in the beginning,
So it is nearer my end [let this be not my ultimate fate].
Teary eyed I watched many lovers depart,
Fiercely mild I drove the rest into the sunset;
A man like me cannot be loved,
A man like me has forgotten how to love,
I am a villain unto myself.
Yet a lover's breast I crave tonight, warriors too
Need tenderness once awhile. Tonight I seek
The strength of a woman, from my breast to hers
Let my burdens journey and be shared,
Then in her tenderness
Lie the night of truth and pray to die in heaven.
May those that are loved cherish the gift,
For between self and sense, love is the rift.

Death Do Part

What shall quench love's thirst but blood?
Here I die to relieve my aching breast!
 As my heart belongs in your hand
So does my blood on your altar,
Now live in knowing that a man pledged life
For your love, bled to colour your rose!
Let petals bloom rained in my blood
And tint your skies and horizons;
When many promise to die for you
Remember that I have, my breath is your prize
When you know your worth: death is life without you.

If my love is returned as much as given,
Follow me by the noose and together
We shall stammer the gods in envy:
They give life yet are incapable of such sacrifice-
Mortal love sworn and bonded in death;
I will scream my love though laden with earth!
With this scarlet rose I take my leap,
Let it be written that I loved you to the end.
Now Death, do your part and seal my truth.

Memoirs Of A Sunset

What is love? To stand at the cremation of the sun
And watch the diffusion of his ashes until darkness has won
Then make promises that through love's downs there will
always be
An up as two wade through time's endless sea?
Or that by prolonged absence through life's seasons
That leaves one dry, the other will return for the simple reason
That brings the rain back to the itching savannah:
It's nature's calling, they belong to each other.
What is love? The meeting of a different heart
To merge like ink and canvas in art,
Two into one diffused to never part
Until the very fabric of being –life- is cut?
If love has night and day let me burn you to ash
To paint the sky of my world, my heart as the brush
That though you be out of light and reach
I can feel you around me closer than a wish,
Then with tomorrow's rebirth of the sun
The journey of a thousand years may have re-begun.

O fair damsel thou hast made me an undesirable in the eyes of
the gods!

As I bleed my vein white upon this page,
By the scrotum of Mercury I swear vengeance!
Hell-sent mercenaries; they rent my love from my arms,
They rent my heart from my breast.
Jealous beings of a higher order,
Immortals envying mortals,
The gods of weeping skies turned slaves of greed,
Greater is the heart I have than the throne of the children of
envy!
My sword in the sky, vengeance in my head,
Tonight, Mercury shall face a mortal pang:
His son's immortal blindness I swear upon his soul.
Love I am coming, the grave that ate shall spew forth tonight!
On this light page I air my dark thoughts:
Breathe dust immortal one!

O fair damsel thou hast made me undesirable in the eyes of
the gods!

The vengeance of love upon my tongue pronounced,
Olympus burns by the hand tonight:
By the hand that paddles me across the Styx,
By the hand that castrates Mercury,
Strangles Cupid and rapes Venus
Until the blind one's sibling is beget!
All is fair in love and war, tonight I deal in both.
Tell them the blade of Hector shall be too blunt,
No warrior shall stand between them and death!
Upon the torso of Apollo my name is carved with an arrow,
Their golden goblets defiled overflow in their blood!
Tell those that took you from me tonight I come to rebuild
Our bilateral heaven on the ashes of Olympus,
Tell those fiends in the sky I am coming…

The Lost Verses

A Proposal

You have a beautiful ~~cunt~~ countenance
And I'm so into you, withdrawal
Is not an option, can I come inside
You heart? By my knowledge of the book of Karma
After you let me come-in you'll be doing all the coming
Around thereafter. Don't like what I'm saying? Leave,
It's the parting that sweetens love,
When you walk away I'll be thinking about your legs.
But the proof of the doodling is in the testing,
Let's make merry, honeymoon tonight
Marry tomorrow, you Mary me Joseph,
Poetry my carpentry, Jesus is my witness;
Ngicabanga wena nxa ng'baza.
Don't read too much into it,
I'm just a punster fucking with your head.

The Gambler

He played hide-and-seek with his conscience,
Catch-me-if-you-can with reality.
He was the cat, flying ahead of the mouse.
The witty mouse on a whole different plane
Drew him to Hell's Gate with hologram goalposts.
Then like the smelted nuggets on Gaddafi's pistols
Amounted to naught when they fried the Colonel,
Glimmering intent fizzled to ash in his hand.
Ironed out by the perfect suit,
What became of the game then?
Black Jack stubs Queen of Hearts,
The latter outshone by Queen of Diamonds,
The trump becomes the gilded queen who kept
His heart in check. His reason too,
Now check: the digger plays six of spades,
Check, nowhere to run, mate.

Good Old Days

I think of those old times dear friend,
Yearning for a beard not knowing its weight,
I think of yesterday frozen dead;
The girls are coming we lie in wait…
Time frozen memories warm my heart,
But times must change with coming age,
How many have we watched depart?
More than I recorded on my page.
Innocence washed and laid to rest,
Can't go out, need to pay the bill.
And she can't come lie in my nest,
The phone company froze my life still.
Illusions of faraway revealed by travel,
It was a lie, fairytales are more true.
Dreams of jets replaced with shovel,
Be glad it's so, we are among the few,
At least we made it out the flame.
Eagerness to scribble consumed by reality,
I'm now too weary to chase fame,
No bread for me, ink a liability,
Palliative care for a death-bound man.
Cancerous memories of innocent love
Consume sanity and all that I am.
Freedom did come at a price,
Forget the past was Her advice,
Yesterday is gone, things will never be the same.

Toil

She said I'm niggardly with my emotions,
Maybe because I am too dark
And a flower must wilt and die, rise again
Before I call it a rose.
Bloodshot eyes, painted by the object in view
That wounded the soul and splattered crimson martyrdom
Across its glass walls. The soul flickers beyond the scar,
Rekindled in affirmation that Purpose in still in control
Beyond these prison walls re-coloured grey with bashed
sanity.
Life clasped in death, fading like Bethlehem's star
Shooting himself to death,
The mind thinks blasphemies the tongue cannot speak
While the dream, cast in concrete
Is choked by the city's unforgiving fist;
My fist size mortar beats insolently.
The soul, threatened with blindness
Clouds the eyes with her sorrow:
But there must be a brighter tomorrow,
There must be sunshine beyond this hail,
There must be a God beyond this hell
To bless this bread buttered in ambition
And washed down with gratitude
Squeezed from blistered feet with toil blackened hands.

Black Salvation

Gold capped tooth, she's from the school of hard knocks,
Gown shorter than a boxer's prize,
No need for a low head to know what's going on under-there.
Lips pursed, morals taxed by sin,
Lust for offering, tobacco incense fumes.
Defiant head cocked back,
Bubblegum pop ricochets off the dance-floor into my ear
As she shoots a wink inviting me to get down,
Bring your wallet, even freewill ain't free,
Ask Nkosi Johnson how much life is worth,
Trade yours for fifty Rands and a five minute writhe.
From candid talk to hotel suites, sugar coated death,
Red lipstick the reaper's scythe,
Jesus won't save you, try a rubber sheath.

Aberration

Spirits mixed into intoxicating concoction
Shared through lips, tender taste of souls,
The lover is a cannibal, instinct animal.
Ravishing creature, fire in her touch,
She felt the skin and torched the soul,
Its ashes, raised like mist in the aftermath of dawn
Cloud all view, the slow sizzling
Of marrow my ultimate surrender.
I fall with her skirts and inhale the incense
Of her loins then taste the salt of her delight,
Ecstasy ignite, tongue flickering in the dance of flames
As pleasure burns. Heaving: air for the fire;
Her gaze to heaven, mine to her fine
Cherubic flair glowing in the flame of passion.
Her ashes diffuse to meet mine in infinity,
We are no longer human when souls are drunk,
Inflamed spirits, rapturous rhythm
Shreds the flesh already bare,
Feline clawing, a purr,
A scream, a whisper, a finger's glide,
Silence…

After Sunset

We made merry beneath a ring of stars,
Enthralled the elements into fantasy;
Entranced, the uncultured step of ecstasy,
You rustled like a leaf in the wind of my palm,
Glowing like a forest ablaze.
Entwined, the rhythm of soul friction
While music watered down spirits that died in lack of
ululation.
Ghosts of yesteryear hovering in our frenzy,
Convulsing to the electricity of the drumming staccato
While the mbira wailed piercingly.
We returned to the beginning
When I was Time and you existence,
When I was silence and you were wind.
I loved you more than when I lost you,
Then the sun came up and it was all over.

If it's parting that sweetens love,
God gave man breath so he could experience death.

City Lights

Stop, halt, chill…
Now breathe the foul stench of Modernization…
The horses that shat were better than these that fart.
I extend my leg to elevate that Achilles tendon that never
healed
On luscious moulds of God's moulding putty
Then grin at the sight of Victoria Exposed.
Grins betray joy and often sarcasm, borrowed happiness
That tried to suppress that yearning for my eyes to burn with
lust
For a damsel trotting along the thorny path
With a water gourd to halo the female deity.
No longer will I know the passion of gods,
To whom creation was a prerogative.
I am a free captive of a time of borrowed limbs,
Egos inflated with penis pumps, and then these borrowed
swords
Break their rubber sheaths and procreate chaos
Which manifests in paper work and maintenance and…
The black man is mauled by the concrete jungle.
He sees a bright light as he walks into the mausoleum.
For fifty Rand he will purchase a coffin. The red light blinds
him
Though it should not hurt for
The fabled lights of heaven are bright but do not harm;
Thus these must be the city lights…

Adam's Dilemma

"Shall I meet her offer with a yes,
Taste the fruit of nakedness?
Take the fruit of leopard's curse,
Prepare all mankind for the depths?
Solitude I cannot bear,
If love is war, then all is fair…"
The voice of truth could not be mum:

Is she worth all the pending harm?

"The birds and trees that birth in pairs
Will forever meet my envy's gaze,
I'll envy flower, I'll envy dove
And curse the day I learnt to love.
Since love has come my way but once
It must be worth this sacrifice…"

Sparring With Youth And Alcohol

The day of death has no telling my people say,
Those who have seen great beasts fall will agree.
What do you know of the mutiny of will and sinew?
Of clawing the earth in helplessness looking for answers in
question?
A man left with his thoughts for too long
Is a liability to his sanity and health.

Last night hell spat me out,
The reaper looked into my eyes and said:
'To die means to have lived,
Return when the chasm is filled...'
I was too drunk to decipher his wordsmith zealotry,
Too interested in the whiskey bottle's harlotry,
And too distant to put a leash on my rabid thoughts;
After a full assault; shot after shot
I was no good at holding anything, especially my liquor.
I wandered into the eternity I promised
And found the One I once cherished.
She hadn't grown taller, just prettier.
I picked the immortal cherry of Her lips and ate my fill,
Her taste hadn't changed either.
Suspended between illusion and memory
Aloud I said the words I often hushed from my heart,
A little strange for a man sitting in the dust.
Vic and Mike picked me up to the bumper of the Jeep,
I was way too gone to answer any of their questions bundled
with my own.
Mother says I drink too much, father says I am his son,
Christened his prince with a Castle at sixteen,
I don't think he knows of my self-destructive episodes...

Struggling with the reality of being my father's son
I paid heavily for my gluttonous indulgence:

I puked my sanity out and landed in it.
Mingled with corn chips, shards of the bottle
I ate more than drank and the saliva of country whores
I saw her again behind my eyelids where longing tattooed her,
Disapproval in her face, cursing the man she loves who
refuses to grow up.
Jack was never a man of principle, kicked me when I was
down
And more horse-piss trumpeted, but then again Jack isn't
really a man…
I had escaped enough episodes of alcohol poisoning
To know what it would be like when I finally cross over.
In the smouldering December dust I lay helpless
Waiting for Anubis to oil me up.
Like every mortal pharaoh I filled my tomb with worldly
treasure;
Happy fragments of my short morbid existence.
I packed Her in multiplicity until She fitted no more
In different forms from the spectacled street walker
To the naked eye gem I alone knew,
Then stiffened at the thought of never seeing Her again
Because all drunkards will go to hell [as I have been told].
I let the fifth or sixth burp out [who was counting?]
And wiped my chin with jacket sleeve,
Clawed the dust in Tshaka defiance and bellowed deep…
To land in the multi-coloured paste again. Willpower is
overrated.
Mummy-wrapped in my tweed blazer I sprawled defeated,
The lights around me dimmed and my laborious breathing
too.
I dreamt of the neat highway and a tiny white Porsche
Speeding away, sparing the accelerator only for the clutch.
Somewhere between that dream and this chronicle I swore
I would never drink again, I have strong suspicions I was
lying to myself,
But all the same, I might not resurrect the next time I die.

Accounting 1-001

From time's purse,
Two faces on the same coin, similar,
But different enough to stand apart
Are cast into the fountain of dreams
Which thirst never slakes,
Into those murky waters where
Our ancestors convulsed their last dance
To the rape of the maxim:
Mzilikazi's trail reduced to a puddle,
Nehanda dragged her dreams on a noose.
The coin will not be shiny for long,
In rust your features redrawn,
My worth tarnished to the shades of those
That came before us,
Devalued in the fountain of dreams that never slakes.

A Cleansing Rain

Dawn is broken,
Heaven has bathed his lover in dew
And crowned her with the glory of Venus.
To their duties larks scurry with madrigals
And ballads, heaven's own compositions.

Man, son of the Earth is risen
To rape his own mother,
He has tamed the Savanna, shaved her bushes clean.
An uMganu tree standing sentinel at the heart of the open
veldt
Nests the birds while grass, the wilderness' defiance
Aspiring to his stature nods to the bees' acapella
Barely audible over the humming of modernization;
The organized rape of the world.

Heaven is incensed, his brow furrows into a scrawl,
Spits lightning and growls thunder.
Man, puny again scurries for safety.
The winds gather to his tempestuous wrath,
Heaven inhales and breathes typhoons.

When it is over fragments of what man hailed
As the epitome of civilization remain with his lifeless form
Splattered across the belly of the Earth. It's all
Ash and dust, soaking into her belly
As the wilderness wakes to new life…

The Coin Of Ntsiri

Horse piss in the belly sank to the bladder,
Slithering and sliding with venomous stealth
To touch the ground as song broke the night.
The blind and the idealists only hear of such,
Pass, accept and squint, pass again,
The one I love is a whore, kisses men and women shamelessly
Trading hands and stirring up long forgotten limbs.
Rough hands, taps of sweat that watered fields touch momentarily
In exchange to drink the bottled sweat of their labour,
Let's drink to a bumper harvest [and make more of this]!
Behold the ancient one, whose lips have told more lies than
Wisdom beneath this teak awaits his turn…his face wrinkles more
And three jagged rocks appear, traces of a smile lost millennia ago.
Whoever said alcohol kills has a mother-in-law among us,
They won't know when he has poisoned her.
I accept a compliment about my eyes
With the quarter-jack of the illegal spew [I know better than to
drink
Flammables but this is a symbol of brotherhood,
People find more between the lines of a blank page
Than in black and white]. Her volley of compliments is succeeded
by great irony: my mother taught her the ABCs yet her second child
is my age,
I am my mother's first.
She points me to her humble abode, half as pretty as her rural self,
I am slipping…I have a rough idea of what's next as the poetry of
drink
Escapes my lips. Before I know it I have pocketed her,
My stories with older women are confirmed by the passion of
drunks
As I deposit the bright coin of moonshine into her jukebox
And sing along…

Away

I dance with madness beneath starlit infinity
And bathe with pretence before I wear the real world.
I knew sanity once, she was twice misleading
And I ended up in the same place,
So I chose her winged sister who bears me beyond the lights
Of her kin and their deep red shades.
She showed me laughter and how the cautious are gullible
In their attempts to define the inevitable.
What is afterlife? 'That which existed before life,'
She answered; 'religion is where love meets fear.
Beyond the realm of reason lives faith,
Love me and I shall carry you beyond both, fear not,
Touch me and I shall show you truth
In all its infinity. To define is to confine,
Thus to say this is the Truth is to lie'.
The black velvet of her grace swept my gaze,
Clothed in the gilt edged night she was majesty,
An elusive presence of right interwoven with wrong.
As her skirts flared with the wind she whispered,
'Freedom, I am freedom from the oppression of your mind;
I am the truth that lurks in the darkness,
The folly of reason…'

Mntaka Nyoko

O ya!
Waze wangikhumbuza kudala
Umhlab' ung'kahlabi:

Amatshe eng'ka ncwebeki,
UNkulunkulu esangumfana;
Usatani eng'kabi lempondo
Ingilosi zisangamatsiyane.

UMuhl' uyaloya,
Esfubeni ang'sela moya,
Seng'fun' ukuzi bambabamba
Ngitshay' ikongonya.

Hayi, ayisikho ebengijong'
Ukutsho, ngesab' amehl'
Abantu lendlebe zomhawu.

Sondela s'angane,
S'thandane, s'engane, s'goqane,
Osehlukanisayo ngokh' imbhabazane!

Okwehlul' oncengayo kweneliswa
Liphane, usufuna ngize
Ngikukatse ukuze ulalele nxa
Ngikwethela lezi nganekwane?!

A Woman's Chore

She heaves and cleaves,
Claws and mourns softly to herself.
Turning her head she sees him behind,
Weary but won't ask for a break,
She'd sooner her back break
For she knows how dispensable
Women like her are to a man like him;
He'll find another to replace her
Sooner than she can walk away.
How much more? Silence pleads,
Speech wrung from the body
In the name of love, sweat pours
From all pores, dribbling to the floor
She has watched all day on all fours
While he stands behind her coaxing
Her feeble body to breaking point.
No worries of disease, God is watching
And He is never cruel she's been taught,
So she'll continue scrubbing these floors
Until her children's wings
Are fully fledged for boundless skies.

Dear Neighbour

I hungered in the night and wandered into the woods
Armed with my spear and a bag for the spoils.
Stealthily I stole away evading viper tongues,
Boa constrictors and cougars in their drool.
I came upon a sleep-drunken dyke,
Negotiated the terrain, then as I lay on my belly
About to stab through the bush where she lay,
Lo and behold, a queer looking fellow while
Bundling his faggot appeared and buggered up my schemes
Before gaily running home to enjoy his cup of tea.
He startled my prey and I shall sleep unfed
If you deny me your neighbourly favour
And a piece of something to see me to bed.

Desert Song

I reach across the void to beg your grace,
These lips where you sit too long too dry.
Lend me a kiss and I my beloved
Will know that heaven is not in my head.
See, nothing I own, nothing mine to give
Only these words to betray my heart;
Honest and true, entirely devoted to you.
In the sun I toil and blister,
Beneath the moon's halo I scab,
Toil I embrace in your name
And I heal in the promise of a new day:
You by my side against the raging tide,
An eye in heaven to look down
At this swelling hell,
I a servant, your will my master.
Dangle a thread o' love, lend me a kiss
And I will feel the spur to edge forth,
The journey's hard but still I trudge,
Oasis or mirage, all I see is you.

Sailing

The beautiful one is leaving,
I cast sight to sea and howl
After the bark stripping us apart.
My weakest part is bare,
My sky darkens, crumbles
And refills the vast blue.
Sail away o' love,
Sail away o' my tears!
But remember me o love,
Remember my eyes
That climbed your form
Tirelessly
Dragging my heart
Across your entire being.
Remember my eyes, beloved,
Sealed forever at your parting.
Forever shunning merriness,
Enshrouded in darkness;
I adore my sadness as a widow
Cherishes her black garments
And clings to them to the
Resurrection of the faithful.
Can none hear me cry
For the promised land
Where I called you
'Honey' and loved you
Beneath the Milky-Way?
I will wait for you, my love,
Wait until that day you shine
On the horizon and grow
As you near your truest home:
My heart that never saw your
Blemishes, but piously
Chanted your name in all
Waking days and rewrote
The babbler's babble.

The Parting

Wherefore dost thou journey my lord?

To nick the devil's treasure
By the edge of the abyss.

My lord?!

Aye, there where evil lurks unveiled,
A thousand terrors uncloaked in her night
Most unknown, for those that eyed them speak no more.

A place most vile my lord!

Most vile and foul indeed,
Devils and horny cuckolds grind horns
And warlocks in skulls of saints gorge their prosperity.
Goblins gobble gall in goblets
And wind touches to defile.

Shalt thou love me still where dew is crimson
And tear much too common for reverence?

By troth, while devils flock and the seraph takes wing,
Hellhounds igniting thunder in the night sky,
I shall with brandished steel forge through,
Raging like a thousand suns 'til Mars cries 'peace! Peace!'
Only to calm my aching breast.

If thou must go, depart thus with fortune to crest thy armour,
But pray, return to mine own bosom,
Shalt thou return my lord, shalt thou?

With the four winds betwixt my thighs
And furrow the earth like hell's steeds in my haste to thee.

Nay my love, nay! Thy beauty is not without, 'tis within,
And that likeness that ignited lyre songs of leering swains
To dust is etched within my heart and traced upon my mind
of purpose. When I see thee there no more then shall I wither
to dust
For I wear thee as a silken garment upon my humble soul.
'Tis for thee I journey, dost thou see how this our lack by the
day
Gains familiarity upon us that these rags unbecomingly
Become us? I promised thee stars for clasps and pearls for
play,
Thus I bid thee adieu with a weeping heart and pregnant
promise
To Caesar-butcher the tyrant and deliver my word's birth
To thee on the morrow by his marrow on my steel.

What I Hoped She'd Say...

I was a girl once and you were a boy.
You told me you loved me and I listened to my heart
That said the same. We were young and dumb,
Yet every moment was worth it.

I was a virgin when I first loved you,
You cradled me close, filled my head with words
And made me feel warm all over,
I have no imagery beyond that.

It was all perfect, right from the first kiss.
It was quite everything I had hoped and imagined,
When the heart believes there is no fear,
When fear died ecstasy prevailed.

I believed everything you told me,
Believed in fate and love as part of the trinity,
So I pledged my nakedness as incense
And virgin blood as a sacrifice.
God remained to be seen.

Entirely devoted to you,
You led me through the plains that you alone knew,
I yielded my youth and innocence to you,
Entwined our souls like tongues.
Snake-charmer, your every word was a song.

You should have stayed my own,
Cradling me like a rose, filling my head with poems,
Alas we just couldn't work,
It wasn't you nor me,
Something greater than what we had.

I had to learn to live apart from you
Though I swore I never could.
Being delusional kept me sane,
How else could I ever be the same?

Just another girl with issues to deal
With before I become a walking stereotype,
Before someone takes advantage and
Turns me into one of his statistics.

The problem with healing is
Getting hurt in the same place again.
That's why he is just like you but
I swear I could be happier,
So this must be purgatory;

Far enough from hell to hear echoes
Of screams, yet close enough to heaven to
Catch a whiff of angel hair.
You should have had the courage to keep me
When you had me.

Since neither of us tried it was your fault,
I thought you would fight for it, for us,
It must not have mattered enough to you
And I would be mad at you if you didn't
Have reasons to think the same about me.

I wish you were dead to me,
Though if you were to actually die
I don't think I would be far behind.
Death is so final,
No chance at being delusional there.

The idea of never loving you again hurts
But the prospect of a repeat is nonexistent.
People change; I hope I wasn't the reason for yours;
Ideally there is a prospect in the future,
Hopefully near, I don't want to wait too long.

Blood And Rain

The last love letter written in blood
Across the skies of desolation,
An echo of the sun bleeding on the horizon
To nothingness, pitch. The loveliest day comes to an end,
Tomorrow I forget you and remember misery,
But tonight's hell is insomnia,
Washing away our made-up reality
In your tears of mascara,
Black as the clouds laden on the sky of eternity
Where our setting sun bled his last defiance in vain.
Here I too wring my thoughts and bleed black drops
To punctuate this love letter;
Poisoned dew on our flower,
Dark as the seed of night now planted in my heart,
Dark as the well whence forth it flows, for
Where the muse goes the art follows.
Black pens tremble to their wake,
Their time has dawned.

Credits:

Edited by: John Eppel
Cover Illustration: Charles Nkomo
Cover Design & logo: Tswarelo Mothobe

ISBN 978-0-620-53446-8

www.ingramcontent.com/pod-product-compliance
Lightning Source LLC
Chambersburg PA
CBHW030830060726

47590CB00004B/1473